Jackie Tales

The Untold Stories of Jack's Sister

Jackie Tales
The Untold Stories of Jack's Sister

Written by: Teri Lott

Cover by Teri Lott & Erin O'Neil

This book is a compilation of original stories and stories that have been adapted from around the world. Names, characters, businesses, places, events, and incidents are either the product of the author's imagination or used in a fictious manner. Thank you to the wonderful storytellers who have influenced the adaptions you will read within this publication.

For all the lovers of stories - the listeners, the readers, and the tellers. And to my hubby, family and friends who kept encouraging me to write a book. Here is my third. Enjoy!

Table of Contents

An Introduction to Jackie – Just Who is She?

Many of you know Jack. Jack, the younger brother of Tom and Will. Jack, the lazy son of Ma and Pa. Jack, the fool who usually comes out on top of things. But do you know Jackie? Jackie, the younger sister of Tom and Will. Jackie, the only daughter of Ma and Pa. Jackie, the fool who usually comes out on top of things. Jackie, Jack's fraternal twin, younger by thirteen minutes.

Now you may be wondering why you've never heard of Jackie. You shouldn't be surprised, after all, in a family of three boys the only girl could easily get overlooked. Well, I'm going to give Jackie the recognition she deserves.

First, let me tell you a bit about Jackie. You're probably wonderin' what she looks like. Well, even though she and Jack are fraternal and not identical twins, if you put a long dark brown wig on Jack, well you've got Jackie. She doesn't win any beauty contests, but she isn't an ugly duckling either.

Jackie squeaked by in school and what she lacks in book smarts she also lacks in common sense. Just like her twin, she is not the sharpest crayon in the box. And clumsy! Pretty much anything Jackie puts her hands on, she drops. It is as if instead of eight fingers and two thumbs she has ten thumbs!

All of this being said, Jackie is different from Jack in that she is always trying to help Ma around the house. She is not lazy like her twin. But being all thumbs means Jackie has dropped and broken a lot of dishware. In an effort to protect what glasses and dishes they have left; Ma usually finds outdoor chores for Jackie to do. That might be the other reason you've never heard of Jackie – she is outside most of the time!

I guess the last thing you need to know about Jackie is she has a kind heart. Sometimes her kind heart overrides the little bit of common sense she has and causes her trouble.

1

Jackie's Winter Friend

The day I'm going to tell you about was a cold day in winter. Well cold probably isn't the best word to describe that day. It was freezing! In fact in was the coldest winter day they had ever seen in those parts. It was a cold that chilled your bones and made them ache. It was a cold that caused your breath to freeze in the air with each exhale. Amazed at this, Jackie, who was outside as usual, started wandering aimlessly in the yard, breathing out and then staring at her frozen breath.

Without realizing it, she had soon wandered to the edge of the wood that lined the back of their property. Suddenly she tripped on something. You've heard the expression, "She has two left feet." When Jackie walked on uneven terrain, it was like she was a centipede with all left feet.

She righted herself and looked at what had caused her to trip. It was a small log. She looked at the log and said, "I'm sorry. I'll put you back where you were."

As Jackie bent to return the log to its place, she saw something under the log. It looked like a pinecone to Jackie, so she reached over to pick it up.

"Owww – eeee!" she screamed. That scream froze in the air. It wasn't a pinecone, of course, a pinecone would not hurt your hand like that. It was actually a baby hedgehog, but Jackie didn't know that.

"Well, aren't you a cutie," Jackie said as she tried to pick it up again. "Owwww – eeee!" she screamed again. "You sure have a painful back side. Well, painful to me anyway."

Jackie thought about her situation for a while and then inspiration hit. She took her scarf, the beautiful scarlet scarf Ma had knitted for her, from around her neck and wrapped it around her hand. Then she gently picked up the little critter.

2

"Where's your Mama, little critter?" The hedgehog just looked up at Jackie with dark, sad eyes. "Let's see if we can find her."

So Jackie started through the woods, tripping over rocks, and fallen logs, but always righting herself and miraculously never dropping the hedgehog.

But as hard as she looked, and she looked for hours, Jackie did not find any critters that looked like the scared creature she held in her hands.

Around noon time, Jackie's stomach began talking to her, "Grrr... grrr." It was letting her know that it was time to head back home for lunch. "Well, we might as well get something to eat and then we can look for your family again," Jackie told the hedgehog. "I always think better on a full stomach," she said laughing. That wasn't true of course, nothing helped poor Jackie think better. Then Jackie noticed the critter had fallen asleep in the warmth of that scarf.

Even though Jackie often did foolish things and was as clumsy as a toddler first learning to walk, she had an unerring ability to always find her way around. She turned in the correct direction and started her trek toward home.

Unfortunately one of her next stumbles caused her to right herself in front of a bear's den. "Ouch!" she cried out. Curious about the sound, but not inclined to stop snoozing, the bear slowly opened one eye. Seeing a tasty meal in front of him, he growled and commenced to pull himself up to his feet.

Jackie wasted no time, she turned and began to run as fast as her bony, bowlegs would allow. But Jackie had never been much of a runner – difficult to do with all those left feet - and the hungry bear was soon catching up.

Now while Jackie had been looking for the hedgehog's family, the sun had come out and the air had begun to warm. And wouldn't you know it, Jackie's path led her and that bear right back to the spot where Jackie had found the little hedgehog.

3

Just as that bear was reaching out his huge paw to grab Jackie's long hair, her first scream thawed. "Owww – eeee!"

Startled, the bear retracted his paw and looked around to find the source of that piercing sound! And then, "Owww – eeee!", the second scream thawed. Well, that bear turned on his paws and ran as fast as his legs would carry him all the way back to his den.

Jackie, oblivious to how close she had come to being a bear's lunch, continued her trek home. She sat down to a delicious lunch of hot cornbread and beans. When Ma asked her what she had done that morning her reply was, "Not much, but I made a new friend." She unwrapped her scarlet scarf and showed them the little hedgehog.

Jack was amazed and asked Ma if she knew what it was. Ma, who was wise about many things including outdoor critters, replied, "Why that's a baby hedgehog and it sure looks hungry."

Jackie started to give her new friend some beans, but her Ma stopped her. "No Jackie, let's give it some pieces of fruit." The hedgehog ate as if it had not eaten for days and then immediately fell back to sleep on Jackie's scarlet scarf. "Well," Ma said laughing, "it looks like I need to knit you a new scarf!"

That's how Jackie got a new scarf and a new friend. She named her friend Harold and the two of them had a wonderful time doing Jackie's chores together. If you ever stop by, you're likely to see Harold on Jackie's shoulder and in Jackie's pocket there's bound to be a grape or two for Harold to munch on.

The Glove

Based on the Ukrainian tale, The Mitten

Jackie was the youngest child in her family. The only girl in a family of three older brothers- Tom, Will and Jack. She was Jack's twin sister, but she was younger by thirteen minutes.

Being the only girl, Jackie was often overlooked. In the winter, Tom, Will and Jack would build a fort and have snowball fights with other boys in the neighborhood, but did they ever invite her to come? NO, they did not! And Jackie could make and throw a mean snowball.

In the spring, her brothers would go fishing, but did they ever invite her to come? NO, they did not! And Jackie knew how to fish. She even baited her own hooks.

During the summer, Tom, Will and Jack would play baseball, but did they ever invite her to come? NO, they did not! And Jackie could throw a baseball and use a bat as well as any of them.

In the fall, her brothers joined other boys and played football, but did they ever invite her to come? NO, they did not! And that was probably just as well because Jackie didn't run well, and she couldn't kick a football very well.

She was a bit clumsy and klutzy – which means she tripped a lot, she dropped things a lot and she fell down a lot.

All of this meant that Jackie spent a great deal of time by herself and even though she would offer to help their Ma in the house, she broke a lot of things, so Ma would usually tell her no thank you, why don't you go out and get some fresh air? Jackie spent a lot of time outside and a lot of time in the woods at the back of their property. The animals in the woods got to know her really well.

Winter had come again, and it was very cold outside. Ma had a basket of gloves and mittens for the boys and Jackie to grab from. The problem was that most of them did not match because Jackie was always losing one or both of her gloves. Ma kept knitting new ones, and Jackie kept losing them.

Well, Jackie's brothers had challenged the boys next door to a snowball fight, so they had grabbed their coats, hats, and mittens. When Jackie got to the basket, there was one matching set of gloves left – gray ones. She put them on her hands and went out the door.

Soon Jackie was in the woods. She walked along smiling at different animals she saw. Or rather at the clues the animals had left for her to see and hear. She saw the bushy black and white tail of a skunk as she ran into the bushes. She heard the "hoot, hoot" of owl as it flew from one tree to another.

Jackie bent down to pick up something from the ground, taking off her gray glove. It was a quill. Something must have frightened a porcupine and it lost one of its quills. Jackie put the quill in her coat pocket and continued on her way. The glove she had taken off fell, unnoticed onto the ground in front of a fallen log.

Later that afternoon, Jackie headed home to help Ma fix dinner for the family. That night several inches of snow fell on the ground. One of the animals had her nose to the ground and she found the forgotten gray glove. "This would be a nice warm place to stay", she thought. So she squirmed inside and made her way into one of the fingers of the glove. It was a tight fit, but the glove stretched and stretched and stretched. Finally all but her black and white tail was in the finger. It was of course the… skunk.

A little while later, another animal found the forgotten gray glove. "This would be a warm place to stay," he thought. So he squirmed his way into the glove and into another finger. It was a tight fit, but the glove stretched and stretch and stretched. Finally all but his tip of his feathered wing was in the finger. It was of course the …owl.

Sometime later, the glove was found by yet another animal. "This would be a warm place to stay," she thought. So she squirmed her way into the glove and into another finger. It was a tight fit, but the glove stretched and stretched and stretched. Finally all but one masked eye and ear tip was in the finger. It was of course the …raccoon.

Early that afternoon, another animal found the forgotten gray glove by bumping into it, blinking his eyes in the bright afternoon sun. "This would be a warm place to stay," he thought. So he squirmed his way into the glove and into another finger. It was a tight fit, but the glove stretched and stretched and stretched. Finally all but his eyes blinking from the light was in the finger. It was of course the … mole.

Later in the afternoon, the glove was found by yet another animal. "This would be a warm place to stay," she thought. So she squirmed her way into the glove and into another finger. It was a tight fit, but the glove stretched and stretched and stretched. Finally all but her busy red tail with white tip was in the finger. It was of course the … fox.

Next, another animal found the forgotten gray glove. "This would be a warm place to stay," he thought. So he squirmed his way into the glove. There were no finger places left, so he stayed right in the palm. It was a tight fit, but the glove stretched and stretched and stretched. Finally all but a few of his spines were in the glove. It was of course the … porcupine.

The next animal to come by sniffed at the glove. "This would be a warm place to stay," she thought. So she pushed her way into the glove. "OUCH!" she cried when she backed into one of porcupine's spines. "So sorry," said the porcupine. "What's going on?" asked the fox as she moved around in the finger so she could see what had happened. "Stop moving around so much deer!" cried the mole, who could see very well in the dark glove.

"Hey," said raccoon. "Hoot, hoot," said owl. "OH NO," said skunk as her nervousness caused her to release some of her smelly smell. "YUCK!" said all the animals as they pushed to get out of the gray glove.

As they pushed and pushed and pushed, the fingertips of the forgotten gray glove split open, and the animals rolled onto the snow. "Pop! Pop! Pop! Pop! Pop!"

Quickly they got up and ran, or in the case of owl, flew, away from the smelly smell as fast as they could. It was quite the hullabaloo!

The next morning, Jackie was out walking in the wood again. Today she had on one gray glove and one red one. She was on a mission as Ma had told her to find the missing gray glove. Before long, Jackie found it. She stuck it in her pocket and headed home.

Imagine Ma's surprise the day she was washing and found that smelly glove with the missing fingers!

Jackie's Spring Surprise

Jackie is Jack's younger twin sister by 13 minutes. If you've never heard of Jackie, I'm not surprised. As the youngest in a family of three boys, Jackie is often overlooked. And due to Jackie's nature, her clumsy nature of having ten thumbs and a multitude of left feet, she spends most of her time outdoors doing chores for Ma and Pa and wandering around.

Spring had finally come to the area around Jackie's family home. The snow had stopped falling weeks ago and small perennials were beginning to poke their heads up out of the soil. Jackie no longer had to chop much wood to heat their home, so she had more time for her wanderings.

On this particular day, Jackie finished chopping the small pile of wood Ma needed for the cook stove and she helped herself to a cool dipper of water from the well. What to do next? She stuck her head into the back door and called out, "Ma, do you need any help in here?" Having suffered through many broken dishes and glasses when Jackie helped, Ma quickly said, "No, no Jackie. You go ahead and take a nice walk before lunch."

So Jackie set off. She had no particular destination in mind, so she just walked. Soon she reached the wood that lined the back of their property. Remembering an encounter with an angry bear that winter, she steered clear of that bear's den. Instead she headed in another direction, tripping over rocks, and fallen logs as she went. Her hedgehog friend, Harold, had stayed home this time as he had opted instead to take a nap amongst the freshly created wood chips.

Jackie continued her trek, stopping now and then to take a whiff of a bed of wildflowers or picking up a leaf and admiring its shape or color. Jackie didn't think of much as she walked, but that wasn't unusual as Jackie never did much thinking.

The sun was shining brightly as Jackie reached down to pick

some tiny violets. She was going to take them home to Ma. Jackie thought they would look pretty on the dinner table and put a smile on Ma's face.

As Jackie stood back up, that brilliant sun was right in her eyes. WHACK! Her forehead had made contact with a low hanging tree branch. "OUCH!" Jackie hollered not so much because it hurt, although it did, but more because it had surprised her. She reached up to touch her head and found a pump knot already forming.

But our Jackie, our clumsy, klutzy Jackie, was used to pump knots, bumps, and bruises so this did not deter her. It did not slow her down. She got up and started on her way again through the wood.

Without warning, Jackie felt a burst of air on her face. It felt as if someone had released the air of a balloon right in front of her. As she turned her head, Jackie saw something moving through the air quite quickly. It was a blur going by her eyes – a red and blue blur.

Jackie didn't hesitate, she followed that red and blue blur. It landed on a lower branch of a nearby tree. Jackie shaded her eyes with her hand, then blinked. She couldn't believe what she was seeing. She blinked again. No, she was seeing it.

What was it? Glistening in the bright sun was a spider's webbing and as Jackie followed it to its end with her eyes, she caught a glimpse of a small figure in red and blue. It was… a tiny Spiderman!

Rushing closer to the tree, Jackie stumbled again. By the time she righted herself, the miniature Spiderman was gone!

"Wow!" Jackie said to no one in particular. "That was unbelievable!" She shook her head and continued her walk through the wood. That's when she heard a sound, no it was more than a sound, it was music. It was very soft, just a bit over a whisper.

Jackie listened closely and heard, "Teenage Mutant Ninja Turtles, Teenage Mutant Ninja Turtles, Teenage Mutant Ninja Turtles. Heroes in a half shell. Turtle power."

Jackie was confused. It was the first time she had ever heard music in the wood. Then she heard it again. "Teenage Mutant Ninja Turtles, Teenage Mutant Ninja Turtles, Teenage Mutant Ninja Turtles…" but Jackie was distracted by a turtle and didn't hear the rest of the song. It was not the usual turtle you see in the woods, but one wearing a blue mask and swinging on a vine. He was there and then he wasn't.

Things were getting curiouser and curiouser thought Jackie. First seeing Spiderman and now a Teenage Mutant Ninja Turtle, Leonardo if she was not mistaken.

She knew who these characters were, after all she read comic books, but what were they doing in the woods? Was there trouble somewhere? And if so, what could tiny versions of these heroes do? Maybe it was just a small problem.

As Jackie was thinking about all of this, not a small feat for Jackie, she heard another sound. It was the voice of Ma calling for her. "Jackie, lunch is ready! Jac-kie!" Jackie opened her eyes and realized that she had been asleep. She got up and started her trek back home.

Had it all been a dream? What do you think?

Jackie's Unusual Day

Jackie, Jack's twin sister, had had a life full of unusual days. What had happened, you ask. Well, one day she lost her gray glove. The next day, she found her glove in the wood. Not unusual, you're thinking. But the found glove was missing all its fingers and had a stinky smell. Very odd, don't you agree?

Another day Jackie had a close encounter with a bear. Luckily, she got away in the nick of time thanks to a few thawed out screams. She also made a new friend that day with a sharp personality.

Yet another time, she had seen a miniature spider web and a glance at an equally miniature Spiderman. Then she heard some music and saw a tiny Teenage Mutant Ninja Turtle swinging by on a vine.

Yes, Jackie's life was full of unusual days. But she was about to experience the most unusual day she'd ever lived through.

It began as most days did, with Jackie offering to help Ma in the kitchen after she had eaten her breakfast and due to her klutziness, Ma saying no thanks and sending her outside. Jackie headed toward the wood to walk. Jackie spent a lot of time in the wood and knew every inch of it. But being clumsy, she still tripped over large rocks and fallen logs.

Her noisy procession through the wood generally kept any animals who might harm her in the distance, but the smaller animals would come up to greet her. They knew her well.

A small white rabbit hopped up to Jackie. Jackie bent down and said, "Hello there." and gave the bunny a scratch between her ears. The rabbit looked up at Jackie seeming to smile at her, and then hopped away.

Jackie's newest friend, the one with the sharp personality, poked his face out of her coat pocket interested in what was happening. It was Harold, Jackie's hedgehog.

Jackie reached into her other pocket and pulled out a single grape. She fed this to Harold. He took it and went back into her pocket. A grape to a hedgehog was much more interesting than a rabbit.

Jackie continued her trek through the woods. A baby skunk came out of the underbrush and made his way over to Jackie. Jackie reached into her pocket again, laid a grape on the grass and moved back a few steps. The black and white critter gobbled down the grape then turned tail running back into the underbrush.

Jackie was enjoying her morning ramblings through the wood but in the twinkling of an eye everything changed. Animals began dashing from their homes in a state of complete panic. At the same time, Jackie smelled smoke in the air. And even Jackie, who had barely graduated from school and had very little common sense, knew where there's smoke there's fire.

Jackie, the girl who spent so much time in the wood, knew the animals were running away from the fire so she simply ran in the opposite direction. She needed to know if anyone was in trouble. For you see, Jackie had the kindest of hearts.

It was a good thing that Jackie ran in that direction for soon she discovered that it was her family's house that was on fire. "Ma, Pa, Tom, Will, Jack," she yelled. "Where are you?" Jackie ran to the barn and grabbed a bucket. She filled the bucket with water from the horse trough.

As she was running back toward the house, she tripped, and the water dumped all over her! "Oh no!" she cried. "Can't I do anything right? Ma, Pa, Tom, Will, Jack??"

Then she heard the best sounds in the world. Those sounds were sweeter than the chirps of baby birds on a spring day - the voices of her family calling to her. She heard, "Jackie, Jackie, we're over here!"

13

It turns out that Sheriff Joe had been heading home and he saw the fire. He had used his car radio to notify the fire chief and then had rushed into the house and started banging on the door. And then Jackie heard the second-best sounds of her life. The sound of sirens.

As Jackie joined her family to stand near the edge of the wood, the volunteer fire department truck pulled up. In mere seconds, men jumped off the truck and started putting out the flames. And although the fire had looked like a blazing inferno to Jackie, thanks to the quick actions and brave work of the firefighters extraordinarily little of the house was damaged.

Relieved, Ma started telling Jackie about how she and the others had gotten out of the house. The smoke had caused the whole family to pass out! The bangin' and hollerin' of Sheriff Joe woke them up and they were able to get out of the house without bein' any worse for wear. The strange thing, Ma said, was that none of them remembered lockin' the door.

Jackie and her family were so thankful. And Jackie declared the firefighters and Sheriff Joe her all-time heroes. But that locked front door always remained a mystery.

Jackie Helps Out

You've probably heard of Jack, the youngest son of Ma and Pa. Jack, the fool. Jack, who somehow always seems to come out on top of things. But have you heard about his twin sister, Jackie?

Jackie is Jack's fraternal twin sister, younger by 13 minutes. She resembles Jack both in looks, although she has long brown hair, as well as in her lack of cleverness. Jackie is also rather clumsy.

Due to her tendency to be a klutz, Jackie's Ma usually found chores for Jackie to do that wouldn't lend themselves to somethin' being broken. Because unlike Jack, Jackie was not lazy, and she was always offerin' to help.

Today, Ma decided to let Jackie help her do the dishes. In the past, many a dish or glass had been broken when Jackie helped, but today Ma needed several pots and pans to be washed. Unbreakable, made of metal – not glass – pots and pans.

Jackie was thrilled! She scoured the sink with Comet, rinsed it well and then began filling it with hot water to which she added several long squirts of Palmolive dish washing liquid. As the sink began to fill, Jackie waved her hand around under the water to start the suds forming. As she made the suds, bubbles started floating into the air. Jackie began to sing, a bit off key, but she was enjoying herself. "There are bubbles in the air, in the air. There are bubbles in the air, in the air."

It was a song that Ma used to sing to Jack and Jackie when they were younger. It made Ma smile. Seeing that Jackie was off to a good start, she decided to go down the lane to take some food to a neighbor who was feelin' poorly. She did this not only to help the neighbor in need, but also because she thought Jackie would do better if her Ma wasn't lookin' over her shoulder. And Ma knew she would definitely feel better if she didn't have to watch Jackie's unique style of dish washin'.

As the sink filled with water and soapy bubbles, Jackie heard a soft sound, "kii, kii, kii." She looked around and saw her little friend, Harold, coming toward her. "Good morning, sleepy head," Jackie said. "Are you ready for some breakfast?" As Jackie got some small, squirmy, juicy looking worms out of a container in the fridge she completely forgot about the sink. She put the worms in Harold's special bowl and put it on the floor.

Harold, her hedgehog, scrambled over to the bowl and ate hungrily.

Jackie watched him for a few seconds, then stood up and headed back to the sink. The soapy water was running over the edge of the sink and onto the floor.

"Oh no!" Jackie cried out - almost as if she were in pain. "I'm making a mess of things again!" At first, she could not think of what to do. It was as if her body was as frozen in place as her brain often was. Harold ran over to the sink area and started to slip and slide in the soapy water. That's when Jackie realized she needed to shut off the water.

Jackie managed to slip and slide her way over to the sink to turn off the water. Then she said aloud, "What am I going to do?" Harold, who had seen her Ma clean the kitchen floor many times before, headed over to the broom closet and impatiently called to Jackie, "KII, KII, KII."

Jackie walked over to the broom closet and looked down at Harold. "You're trying to tell me something, aren't you fella?" She looked and looked and looked at the door of the broom closet and then a glimmer of an idea entered her brain.

"Of course," Jackie exclaimed, "Ma's mop! You sure are clever, my friend." She reached down and patted Harold's head with one finger.

Jackie got the mop and bucket out of Ma's broom closet and began mopping up the sudsy water. While she was at it, she went ahead and cleaned the entire kitchen floor.

First, she ran the mop through the sudsy water singing another one of her childhood songs, "Wash, wash, wash the floor. Wash it really good. Wash, wash, wash the floor. Wash it as I should." Then Jackie filled the bucket with clean water. Now most of us would rinse out the mop and use it to rinse away the suds, but that was not Jackie's way. She tied sponges to her feet. She poured some of the clean water onto the floor and went sliding along mopping up the sudsy water.

While she waited for the floor to dry, she went outside and played with Harold. They played throw and catch hedgehog style. Jackie would roll an acorn toward Harold. He would pull himself into a ball and roll into the acorn sending it back toward Jackie. His accuracy was amazing, especially when you consider that he couldn't see what he was doing while rolled up.

The acorn went back and forth, back, and forth, until Jackie remembered her original chore – to wash the dirty pots and pans.

Jackie went to the kitchen door and bent down to touch the floor. It was dry. So she headed over to the sink. To her pleasant surprise, the pots that had been in the sink all this time were practically clean. She only had to scrub a few places and then rinse them off and dry them. She was just putting them away when Ma came back from the neighbor's house.

The first thing she noticed was that her kitchen was tidy. That was a relief and she actually let out a happy sigh. Then Ma noticed that the floors were not only clean, but shiny. Jackie was so busy putting pots and pans away that she had not noticed that Ma had come in. Ma said, "Jackie…" but got no further. Jackie screeched and dropped the pot that was in her hands. It banged onto the floor and Harold rolled up into a ball and rolled out of the kitchen.

"I'm sorry, Ma," Jackie said. "Oh, Jackie. No, I'm sorry. That was my fault, honey. I startled you. But no worries, the pot is fine. It just has one more dent." Then Jackie and Ma said together, "It just shows it is loved!"

And that was the day, the truly rare day, that Jackie helped out and everything turned out fine!

Jackie's Mother's Day Gift

You may have heard of Jackie, Jack's twin sister, younger by thirteen minutes, and just as foolish as Jack. If you haven't heard of her, I'm not surprised. Being the youngest girl in a family of three boys, Jackie was often overlooked. But I've made it my goal to tell people about Jackie, the clumsy but kind younger sister of Tom, Will and Jack.

This is one of my stories about her. It's about the time when Jackie was determined to get a gift for her mama for Mother's Day.

Now Jackie wasn't a particularly good planner and since one of her days was much like another, she rarely looked at the calendar that hung on the wall. But she had noticed that her twin brother Jack had been mighty secretive the last few days. When he finally lighted long enough for her to talk to him, she asked, "Whatcha been up to?" "Well," said Jack, "I found out from Tom and Will that Mother's Day is just a few days from now. I've been tryin' to find a gift for Mama." "A few days from now – why didn't you tell me!" said an exasperated Jackie. "Have you found a gift yet?" "Not yet. How about you?" asked Jack. "I didn't even know it was almost Mother's Day 'til just now. I'll have to think of somethin' fast," was Jackie's reply.

Well Jack had his thinkin' spot, a boulder way off in a clearing in the woods and Jackie had hers – the crick that ran through the woods. Jackie went off to the crick right away, took off her dirty Keds and socks and started wading in the cool ankle high water.

As she walked through the water, she smiled at the sound of the birds chirping overhead and the frogs softly croaking nearby. Suddenly, her foot landed on something bumpy and a bit sharp.

"Ouch!" Jackie cried out, more from being startled than from being hurt. She reached down into the water and pulled up a rock.

18

But this rock was unlike any other she had ever seen. It was bumpy with a few sharp jagged spots, but it also shined in the bits of sun that made its way through the trees. Shiny, sparkly, and golden in color. Could it be?

Jackie jumped out of the crick and dashed through the woods and into the meadow. She held the rock up into the bright sunlight. Yep, shiny, sparkly, and golden in color. It must be gold! After all this crick came from a nearby river which everyone said flowed from the foothills of the Appalachian Mountains. And everyone knew gold comes from mountains!

Jackie was delighted! She could give this to mama for Mother's Day. But not the way it was. What good to Mama would a big piece of rocky gold be?

Jackie knew what to do. She'd take it to Mr. Henry who owned the general store. Mr. Henry knew how to do a lot of things. She just bet he could break that rock into two pieces and put a hole into one of them. Then Jackie could give them to Mama as a pendant to hang on her gold chain and as a broach after Jackie glued a safety pin on the back.

Jackie was so excited that she almost forgot to go back to the crick and get her shoes and socks. But Mama had drilled it into Jackie's head to always wear her shoes and socks into Mr. Henry's store. "It's okay to go barefoot around the house, but you're too old to go into the store with bare feet Jackie," Mama had said over and over again to her. So Jackie dried her feet on the grass and soon her feet were appropriately attired.

Jackie raced to Mr. Henry's store tripping over rocks in the road as she went, once almost ending in a face plant. But finally, out of breath and red faced, she reached the store. Luckily, Mr. Henry had no customers at that moment, so he was able to give Jackie his full attention.

She whispered in an excited voice, "Mr. Henry, Mr. Henry." Mr. Henry looked at Jackie and said, "Take a breath Jackie and calm down."

So Jackie took a deep breath in and out as her Mama had shown her. "Now, what's got you so excited, Jackie?" asked Mr. Henry.

Jackie looked around to make sure no one else was listening in or looking on, and she opened her hand to show Mr. Henry her treasure, "Gold," she said in a loud whisper. Mr. Henry immediately recognized what Jackie had. He shook his head, and, in a calm, soothing voice said, "No Jackie. That's not real gold."

"Oh but it is," Jackie replied and continued in machine gun rapidity, "I found it in the crick and the crick flows from the river and that river comes the Appalachian Mountains, and gold comes from the mountains. I'm gonna give it to Mama for Mother's Day."

"Jackie," Mr. Henry started again in his calm voice, "the gold found in the Appalachian Mountains has all been in the southern states, not here in Ohio. This here is fool's gold. It looks like gold, but it's just a shiny rock." That's when he saw Jackie's face. He hurriedly went on, "But I think your mama would like it just the same." Jackie grinned and told Mr. Henry her plan. He said he thought he could turn it into a small pendant with enough left to make a broach as well.

On Mother's Day, the whole family gathered. After eating mama's wonderful dinner of fried chicken, mashed potatoes and gravy, green bean casserole, cornbread, and homemade pies they shared their gifts with her. She was delighted with everything she received and said she was the luckiest mama in the world.

Later, after the dishes were done and everyone was sittin' on the back porch talkin' and enjoyin' the setting sun, Jackie looked at the pendant hangin' around her Mama's neck and the broach pinned on her sweater. "You know Mama," Jackie said quietly, "those aren't real gold. Mr. Henry told me it's called Fool's Gold."

"That's okay, Jackie," said Mama. "They're just as precious to me as real gold." "Why's that, Mama?" Jackie asked. "Because they're from you, Jackie. They are a gift from you, my darlin' daughter." And Jackie smiled.

Summertime and the Livin's Easy, or Is It?

Now Jackie knew that Ma and Pa were strugglin' to make ends meet and she wanted to do somethin', anythin' to help. But as I may have mentioned, Jackie wasn't real smart and was also hampered with being a klutz. It was hard to find anyone willin' to give her a job, especially when so many men with families to support needed jobs.

It was Ma who actually gave Jackie the idea of a service she could offer people. The afternoon that Jackie came home with her new friend, Harold the Hedgehog, Ma had said, "My goodness Jackie. I've never seen anyone who loves animals as much as you. And they seem to love you back." Jackie thought that being a pet sitter would be a good job for her. You know, someone who takes care of your pets if you have to go out of town on business or if you are lucky enough to take a vacation.

First Jackie made a sign. It said, "Got someplace to go? I will take care of Kitty or Fido." She had thought of the rhyme herself and was proud of it. Ma had helped her with the spelling. She put the sign out in front of their house near the road. Pa saw her sign and said, "That's a good sign, Jackie. Why don't you make one and ask Mr. Henry to put it in his store window? That way more folks will see it." So Jackie made another sign and did just that.

Later that day, Jack saw the sign. He said, "Humph. Nobody is gonna pay you to watch their cats and dogs. They'll just put them outside while they're gone."

Hmm… Jackie hadn't thought about that. She went in to talk to Ma about it. Ma said, "Now some folks will do that, but others won't. I think the main problem is gonna be that most people won't have the cash money to give you. If you are willing to take somethin' else for payment, like eggs or homemade bread, it might just work. You might also want to add that you'll watch their children too. You're just as good with kids as you are with animals," Ma said with a smile.

21

So Jackie made another sign. "Kid sittin' and pet sittin' by Jackie." She didn't take it in for Ma to see, she just put it out front and took another one to Mr. Henry's store.

Well, the sign worked. Just a few days later Jackie had a job! She was delighted! It was at Miz Taylor's house who lived on the other end of the holler from Jackie's family. Miz Taylor was the mistress of all things baked. She made delicious cakes, pies, cookies, and breads. Wonderful smells were always wafting out of her kitchen window. If the wind was just right, they made it to Jackie's house too.

Since this was a job, Jackie arrived wearing her favorite coveralls which were fresh off the clothesline and smelled like the wind and the sun. But before she had left home, Jackie had taken a couple of minutes to restuff her pockets with a few necessities - a long piece of string, several plastic bags in various sizes from the Walmart, her favorite marbles, and a shooter, a yo yo, and a few other essentials.

Jackie knocked on Miz Taylor's back door. Miz Taylor was in the kitchen and called out, "Come on in, Jackie. Girl you are gonna be a lifesaver for me today." Jackie barely had the chance to say, "Howdy" as Miz Taylor went right on talkin' like a fire engine on its way to a fire. "I bet you know that my girl, Betsy Sue, is gettin' married this Saturday." "Yes, ma'am, I did," Jackie managed to squeeze in.

"Well I'm makin' her weddin' cake and I need a few hours of peace and quiet so I can concentrate on gettin' all the fancy frostin' and decorations on. I want you to watch the boys. Take 'em down to the crick, take 'em into the woods, whatever. Keep 'em busy until lunchtime." "Yes, Miz Taylor. I'm sure we'll have fun together. Where are they now?" "I think they're out in the barn," was Miz Taylor's reply.

So out to the barn Jackie went. It was so quiet that Jackie could hear the wind whistlin' through the cracks in the walls.

Jackie knew the boys were hiding just waiting to jump out and scare her. Now Jackie didn't mind being scared, but she wasn't gonna make it easy for them. She dug deep into her pocket and pulled out her marbles and shooter. Taking her right foot, she scraped a circle in the dirt floor. Then down she plopped. She placed the marbles in the center of that circle and putting her shooter between her thumb and pointer finger made her first shot. This was not the usual way to shoot marbles, but it worked for Jackie.

The next thing Jackie knew, three voices were all were all saying, "Can I go next?" And there were the boys – Joey, Andy, and Virgil – out of their hiding places. "Well," Jackie said, "Howdy boys. How bout we have a competition? I'll play Virgil, then whoever wins can play Andy and whoever wins that game will play Joey." The boys thought this sounded fair and so they began. And who do you think was the winner? Yep, it was Jackie. After all, anybody left to their own devices as much as Jackie was, had plenty of time to practice.

After that Jackie took the boys down to the crick. They jumped from rock to rock to rock, back and forth, back, and forth. Jackie had just jumped to the middle rock when her foot slipped on the mossy side, and she fell in. Now you or I might be mad or even feel a bit sad, but not Jackie. She started laughin'. She laughed so hard that the boys came over and started laughin' with her. Before you could say, "Jackie Robinson" Joey, Andy and Virgil sat right down in the cool crick water too. "Splish, splish, splish."

Jackie looked at them, shook her head and said, "We might as well take off our shoes and socks and put them on the crick bank to dry." And so they did. Then she had them scoot up onto the rocks so their shorts would dry out too.

Those three boys and Jackie sat on those rocks in the middle of the crick with their feet in the cool, cool water. Then they all started laughin' again when a school of tadpoles came by and tickled their toes.

It didn't take long for the backsides of their shorts to dry, and Jackie announced it was time to head home for lunch. Now she didn't wear a watch but was used to telling time by lookin' up at the sun. Besides, she could hear four stomachs complainin' – hers and the three boys. They shoved their somewhat damp socks inside their shoes, tied their shoelaces together and flung the shoes over their backs.

23

When they arrived home, Miz Taylor was delighted. The wedding cake was done, and she had had time to make a wonderful lunch of thick peanut butter and homemade strawberry jam on freshly baked bread. Jackie ate her fill and told Miz Taylor it was time for her to head home. Miz Taylor said, "Well Jackie, I appreciate you keepin' the boys busy this mornin' and I'll be tellin' others about your good work. Here's two jars of fresh cream for your help."

Well, Jackie was tickled – not pink, Jackie could never abide the color pink, but tickled. Pa and Ma used cream in their coffee when they could afford the luxury, so this would be a nice treat for them. But it was a scorching hot August day, you know the kind that people say you could fry an egg on the sidewalk kind of day? And the sun beating down on Jackie caused that cream to curdle. Of course Jackie didn't know that, but Ma sure found out when Jackie grinning handed her the two jars.

Ma opened one of the lids, saw the curdled cream and said, "Land sakes, Jackie! You know we keep cream in the ice box. If someone gives you somethin' like cream that can't take the heat, dip it down in the cold-water spring, put it in one of those plastic bags I know you keep in one of your overall pockets and then hurry on home. Please try to remember."

"Yes Ma," Jackie said. "I'll try." Luckily, I can use it tomorrow morning when I churn butter." Jackie smiled. She was proud that she had been able to help out her Ma and Pa.

Well, Miz Taylor was true to her word. The next time she was at Mr. Henry's general store she told everybody how well Jackie had kept her boys busy so she could get some work done. "And none of them got hurt?" asked Miz Baker, who knew of Jackie's proclivity for accidents and general klutziness. "No, no, they were fine," said Miz Taylor. "They came back a bit damp, but all of their important parts were in the right places, and they had a good time."

This gave Miz Baker somethin' to think about. You see, Miz Baker was the mistress of all things sewn. Not only did she make gorgeous gowns and dresses from beautiful new material, but she also reworked old dresses, aprons and, yes, even sheets and pillowcases to make wonderful new clothes. She was a magician with a needle and thread!

Now Miz Baker's son Rodney was marrying Betsy Sue Taylor. So Betsy would soon be Betsy Sue Baker – cute, huh? - and Miz Baker was trying to finish sewing the lace onto Betsy's wedding dress. A few days later, Miz Baker offered Jackie her second job opportunity. She hired Jackie to "amuse the fellas." "The fellas" were Miz Baker's dogs- all six of them!

Jackie was thrilled to have the opportunity to "amuse the fellas." I might have mentioned she loved animals and animals loved her. So she grabbed the lead of the two beagles, the hound dog, the terrier, the sheep dog, and the collie.

They started out walking at a nice pace and Jackie was able to control all six of "the fellas" until they caught a whiff of something. That's when this calm pack became wild and crazy! They pulled Jackie down the holler and into woods. You have to give Jackie credit, she never let go of a single lead! Before she knew what was happenin', "the fellas" had treed a coon.

What a commotion they made! They were barking and howling and baying at that poor creature.

Now you or I might have panicked, but not Jackie. She looked up at that coon and said, "Sorry about this, Rocky." Then she reached into one of the pockets of her overalls, pulled out an object, gripped the six leads tightly and said, "Ball!" as she threw an old tennis ball in the other direction.

Immediately the coon was forgotten. After all, it was now an inanimate object out of reach. Those dogs took out after that ball using their highly trained noses. Once they located that smelly ole ball, Jackie simply said, "Release" to the dog who had it, picked it up and threw it in the direction of home again. Since Jackie was intentionally throwing the ball short distances, it took quite some time before they were back home.

Once they got to Miz Baker's Jackie simply called into the house, "Hello, Miz Baker. We're back. Do you need more time to finish?" Miz Baker called back, "No, Jackie. I just finished up. Come on in. Leave the fellas outside, please."

Jackie went into the house and there it was – a crisp white satin gown covered in the whitest lace she had ever seen. It was breathtaking, even for our Jackie whose usual dress of choice was overalls and a t-shirt. "My that's an awful pretty dress," Jackie told Miz Baker. "Well thank you," Miz Baker replied. "I think it will suit Betsy Sue." "Yes, ma'am, it sure will."

"Well," said Miz Baker, "I thought you might like this little critter as payment for your help today." Miz Baker was holding up the cutest little tiger kitten.

"Ohhh…" said Jackie, "he's adorable. Can I really have him?" "Yep, and thanks for all your help. I hope the dogs weren't too much of a nuisance." "Oh no, we did just fine," said Jackie.

Jackie started home thinking about a name for her new kitten. She noticed a drip of sweat come down from her forehead. That reminded her of what Ma said. "Oh my, goodness. It's too hot for you," she said to the kitten.

So she dug down in her pocket and pulled out a plastic Walmart bag. She put the tiger cat in the bag and dipped it down into the cold-water spring. As she held the bag by its handles, Jackie headed home. Luckily Miz Baker lived just a few doors from Jackie. And luckily for the kitten, Ma knew what to do. I'm happy to tell you that the kitten survived.

After saving the kitten, Ma looked at Jackie and said, "Land sakes, Jackie. You almost killed the little thing. You should have taken bit of string out of pocket and made a collar, then had it follow you home on its "leash." Please try to remember." "Yes Ma," Jackie said. "I'll try."

"Well," Ma said, "This kitten will be a great mouser when it gets a bit older. It's a nice addition to our family." Jackie smiled. She was proud that she had been able to help her Ma and Pa.

Jackie's third job came almost immediately – the next day as a matter of fact. I might have mentioned that Mr. Henry had a general store. The general store was two doors down from Jackie's house if you were headin' down the holler and two doors up from Jackie's house if you were headin' up the holler.

But it was actually his wife, Miz Henrietta, that hired Jackie. It was inventory time at the store, but they had to keep the store open while doing it. You see, they couldn't afford to close the store and besides which there was no other store close by for folks. But often folks brought their kids or dogs into the store with them, so Miz Henrietta was always busy keeping them occupied so their folks could give Mr. Henry their order and he could fill it uninterrupted.

After hearing that Jackie had entertained Miz Taylor's boys and Miz Baker's fellas, Miz Henrietta sent for Jackie. She wanted Jackie to entertain any of the kids that came into the store with their folks so Miz Henrietta could work on the inventory in peace while Mr. Henry waited on the adults. And if someone brought in a dog or cat, Jackie could keep them occupied too.

Jackie was excited about being hired again. Miz Henrietta showed her a chair by the pot-bellied stove that she could sit in until her "services" were needed. She also put a crate next to Jackie that contained a checkers game, some spinning toys, a deck of Go Fish cards, and a few old tennis balls. Jackie was set for whatever and whoever came her way.

For the first few hours, the only folks who came into the store were old men on their own. Mr. Henry was actually able to help Miz Henrietta with some of the inventory. Jackie was beginning to wonder if she would ever have anything to do to earn a salary. But round eleven o'clock, a woman came in with two little girls – one holding her left hand and one holding her right. Mr. Henry came up to the counter and asked, "Can I help you ma'am?" "Yes," she said. "We are on our way to our new place near Plattsville. My husband is already

27

there workin'. I saw your store and since I don't know how close a store will be to our house, I thought I'd stop here."

"Well, we are very happy to serve you," said Mr. Henry. "If your house is on this side of Plattsville, this will be your closest store. If your house is on the other side; you'll want to shop at the new Walmart." "Well, thank you for tellin' me," said the women as one of her children pulled on her arm and the other one whined, "I'm tired, Mama."

Jackie jumped up out of her chair to help with the young'uns. She jumped up so fast, she knocked the chair over. Both of the children looked over her way and stared wide eyed. Jackie said, "Whoops!" and laughed. The children laughed too and started over her way. "Let's play while your Ma shops, okay?" Jackie said. Their Mama let out an audible sigh of relief when she saw that her girls were in good hands. "Do you always have someone here to mind the kids?" she asked Mr. Henry. "It's somethin' new we're tryin'," was his reply. "Well, if you decide to continue it, I'll be shoppin' here all the time." And while Mr. Henry filled her order, Jackie played hide and seek with the two children.

They all had fun and Jackie only knocked over one other thing. Unfortunately, it was a barrel of apples, and those red pieces of deliciousness began to roll here and there and everywhere. But it made the girls laugh and Jackie turned picking them up into a game.

In no time at all, the family's order had been filled and the family waved goodbye. As the day progressed, no one else came in with children or pets so Jackie didn't have anything else to do. Miz Henrietta looked up from her paperwork and said, "Jackie, you did a mighty good job with those girls. Since you live nearby, would you like to work here on an on-call basis?" "I don't know," said Jackie, "What does on-call mean?" Miz Henrietta chuckled and said, "Well, honey, that means if someone comes in with kids, I'll just open up the back door and call for you. If you're free you come on over. On-call." "That sounds good to me," said Jackie delighted that she was going to have a regular job.

Just as Jackie was about to leave, Miz Henrietta handed her three apple and three cherry fry pies as payment for her help. Jackie thanked her and walked out the back door. Then, rememberin' what Ma had said, she pulled a length of string from a pocket and tied each fry pie onto the string. Then she dragged those fry pies home.

When she got home, she grinned at her Ma, telling her she had a good time playin' with two cute little girls at the store. She was just about to tell her about being "on-call" when Ma saw the string she was holdin' onto. Her eyes followed the string to the floor and then to the six fry pies. "Land sakes, Jackie! We can't eat fry pies that have been drug over the ground. You should have asked Miz Henrietta to put them in a bag for you. Oh well, I guess we can mash them up and feed them to the pigs. They like sweet things too."

Jackie smiled. She was proud that she had been able to help out her Ma and Pa. Then she smiled even more as she told her mom that she now had a "regular job". And Ma, well she was smilin' too, proud of her Jackie.

The Barn Dance

For young women like Jackie, average looking gals who, umm …how do I say this nicely, who aren't the brightest bulbs in the lamp, getting an invitation to a dance does not happen every day. So Jackie was pleasantly surprised when a handwritten invitation arrived inviting her to the fall barn dance. It was from a boy she had known since she was in elementary school – Homer.

Now for most girls an invitation from Homer would not be a pleasant surprise. Homer's parents must have known that their son would not be the most handsome of young men – in fact, he was a bit homely in appearance – when they named him Homer. It didn't help that Homer kept his hair cut so short that his ears stuck out of the side of his head. Any jackrabbit would admire his ears. But Jackie didn't care what Homer looked like, he had invited her to the barn dance. She had never been invited to a dance before.

She raced through the house with the invitation in her hand, calling out, "Ma, Ma, Ma." Ma came rushing, wondering what Jackie had broken this time, hoping she had not injured herself. She slowed down when she saw the paper that Jackie was waving around in the air. "Jackie, Jackie, I'm right here. Watch out for the…" CRASH! Jackie had tripped over the footstool that Pa used to elevate his sore feet in the evenings. Luckily, she was okay.

"Ma," she said a bit out of breath, "I got an invite to the barn dance." "You did! Oh, that's great honey," her ma said. "Who invited you?" "Homer," Jackie replied with a smile as wide as the Ohio River and a dreamy look in her eyes. "That's nice," her ma said in a voice that did not quite match her words. "Oh, but Ma," Jackie said as her smile disappeared into thin air, "What will I wear?"

Ma thought about Jackie's wardrobe. It consisted mostly of jeans, shorts, and t-shirts. Her two dresses that she wore to church services, weddings and funerals had seen better days.

"Well," Ma said, "The dance is several weeks off. I'll make you a new one." "Oh, Ma, could you?" asked Jackie as she wrapped her arms around her ma in a bear hug. Ma gasped a bit as she returned Jackie's hug and said, "I will if you don't squeeze the life out of me first!"

"Well," Ma continued as Jackie released her, "I've got most of my chores done for the day. Let's go to Mr. Henry's store to look at material before the day gets away from me and it's time to start supper."

As Ma went into the kitchen to look in the cigar box where she kept her housekeeping money, Jackie ran to her room to look through her own cigar box where she kept her treasures. She found the tortoise shell comb that had been left to her by her Grammy, several marbles, special crystal rocks, an arrowhead – Jack wasn't the only one who collected them- and two dimes and a nickel. Jackie slipped the money into the pocket of her shorts.

"Remember to wash your hands and face and run a comb through your hair!" Ma called out. "Yes, ma'am," Jackie replied. She raced to the bathroom, stumbling over her bedroom door threshold, and sliding on the hall rug all the way to the bathroom. "Wee!" Jackie called out, looking like a surfer catching a big wave! As she cleaned up and pushed the rug back into place, she decided this would be her new way to the bathroom. Fun and quick!

She met Ma at the front door, and they began their short walk to Mr. Henry's store. Jackie was so excited, she bounced along the gravel road. Ma kept lookin' at her and grinnin'. She was almost as excited as Jackie! After all, Jackie was her only daughter, and she rarely wanted a dress – let alone a new one!

They got to the store in no time and Jackie ran up the steps two at a time, tripped and bumped her head on the screen door. Not stopping to even say so much as ouch, she pulled the door open, raced to the counter and said,
"Mr.HenryI'vebeeninvitedtothebarndanceandneedmaterialforanew dressMaisgonnamakeme."

31

Mr. Henry, who knew Jackie well, smiled and said, "Ok, Jackie. Take a deep breath and slow that down a bit. Couldn't understand a word you said." Jackie took one breath – but it wasn't a very deep one – and said…
"I'vebeeninvitedtothebarndanceandneedmaterialforanewdressMais gonnamakeme."

"One more time, Jackie," Mr. Henry said. "Take three deep breaths this time." So Jackie took one, two, three deep breaths and said, "I've been invited to the barn dance and need material for a new dress Ma is gonna make me." "Well now, isn't that something," Mr. Henry said, "Do you know what color you'd like?"

Ma, thinking about Jackie's proclivity to trip, fall and bump things, said, "How about a dark color like navy or red?" "Oh no, Ma," Jackie said, "I want yellow. It's my favorite color," she said turning to Mr. Henry. And before Ma could say anything else, Mr. Henry got on his stepladder and pulled down two bolts of fabric. One was a pale yellow and the other had a white background with small yellow sunflowers scattered all over it.

"That one!" squealed Jackie as she pointed to the sunflower fabric. "I love sunflowers! They are my favorite flower! And they're yellow too!" What could Ma say? Jackie was so thrilled about this fabric, and it was wonderful to see her daughter excited about something other than rocks, arrowheads, and critters.

While Ma was figurin' how much fabric she needed, Mr. Henry covertly slipped off the price tag. Ma said, "How much for three yards, Mr. Henry. I think three yards will be enough." Jackie hoped they could afford the lovely fabric. As she waited for Mr. Henry to tell them, she held her breath, crossed her fingers, and tried to cross her toes, but that kept making her tip over, so she stopped.

"$1.50," Mr. Henry replied. "Oh, I don't have $4.50," Ma responded her voice reflecting the sadness her face showed. Jackie piped up, "I've got twenty-five cents Ma!" As Ma was about to explain that still wasn't enough, Mr. Henry cleared his throat and said, "You misunderstood me, ladies. The cost for three yards is $1.50." "Oh, I don't think so," Ma said as she ran her fingers over the fine quality poplin. "I'm sure it's at least $1.50 a yard." Mr. Henry grinned at Ma, then grinned at Jackie. "Well, I'm having a barn dance sale. Three yards for the price of one!"

And that's how Jackie had a beautiful white dress with small yellow sunflowers to wear to the barn dance. At least it was white when Homer picked her up and they began the walk to the dance.

Just an hour before, Ma had helped Jackie get dressed and had combed her long brown hair until it was as shiny as the coat of their neighbor's Chestnut pony. Then Ma put Grammy's tortoise shell comb in Jackie's hair. It looked perfect!

All that was left was to wait until Homer came. At first Jackie was pacing across the living room, but after she tripped on Pa's footstool and bumped into the end table, Ma made her sit down. Jackie commenced to tapping her foot and Ma was about to tell her to stop when there was a knock at the door. "H-he, he's h-h-ere," said Jackie scarcely able to breath. "Take a deep breath, Jackie, and calm yourself. I'll get the door," Ma instructed.

So Jackie took three deep breaths and the next thing she knew, Homer was standing next to her in the living room with a grin as wide as the Ohio River on his face. "Are you ready, Jackie?" he asked as he reached out his hand.

Jackie stared at his hand and then realized she was supposed to take it. "Umm…yeah, I'm ready," she finally replied. "You sure look pritty," Homer said, still grinnin'. "Thank you," Jackie said.

The two of them said goodbye to Ma and started walking down the path toward the barn dance. Both of them were a bit socially awkward, so the conversation on the way wasn't very scintillating. Finally Homer said, "Umm…I like your dress."

"Thank you," replied Jackie. Then after a while, she added, "My ma made it for me." They walked a bit more in silence when Jackie said, "Umm… you look nice tonight." "Thank you," replied Homer. And then he added, "My ma gave me a haircut." Before there were any more awkward silences, they arrived at the dance.

The music spilling out of the barn was lively. A local group of boys who had just started a band had been hired. They had a guitar player, a fiddle player, a bass player, and a banjo player who also played the harmonica. The lead singer wasn't too bad, although his range was limited, but each band member played their instrument extremely well. So overall the sound was first-rate.

Homer, with that wide grin still on his face, led Jackie right out to the dance floor. It amazes me that although Jackie had two left feet, she seemed to be able to dance with ease. Some things in this world are a wonder, aren't they? Well Homer and Jackie danced several numbers until the band took their first break. "Umm… would you like some punch?" asked Homer. "Yes, please," Jackie replied.

As Homer headed back carefully carrying two very full glasses of Hawaiian punch, Jackie heard someone call out her name. She spun around on her feet to see who was callin' her, just as Homer's outstretched arm was handin' her the punch. Jackie bumped into his hand and the punch flew into the air and showered down on Jackie's new dress. "Oh no!" Jackie cried out. Homer stood there stunned. "I – I - I'm sorry Jackie. It was an accident." "I know, I know," said Jackie. "Oh, why does this always happen to me!"

The punch created pink stains in various places on Jackie's dress as she stared down at it. Someone brought over paper towels and the little bit of punch that missed Jackie's dress was cleaned up off the floor. That same someone handed Jackie paper towels and she wiped off her arms, but there wasn't anything she could do about the stains on her dress, so when the band came back from their break, she told Homer they might as well dance some more.

Surprisingly, at least to me, the rest of the dance went off without a hitch. After the band played their last number, Homer and Jackie began to walk home. Again, there was little conversation between them. Homer attempted to apologize to Jackie about her dress again, but Jackie stopped him saying, "Homer, you might as well know, these kinds of things happen to me all the time. It's not your fault." The rest of the way home was walked in silence, but it was a comfortable silence between two young people who weren't used to small talk.

When they arrived at Jackie's house, Homer leaned over and gave Jackie a quick peck on the cheek, turned quickly and said, "I had a nice time, Jackie." and then he ran down the driveway out onto the road.

Jackie smiled, touched her cheek, and opened the front door tripping over the threshold as she entered. Hearing this familiar sound, Ma came into the living room from the kitchen, wiping her hands on her apron. The first thing she noticed were the pink splotches on Jackie's dress. She was about to say something but then she saw the smile on Jackie's face. Being the wise woman she was, Ma said nothing as Jackie walked up the stairs in a dream-like state, tripping over every second or third step and opening her bedroom door.

That night, Ma went into Jackie's bedroom and gathered up the white dress with yellow sunflowers and pink splotches. The next time Jackie saw that dress, it was a pale pink dress with yellow sunflowers. Jackie was thrilled as the pink color reminded her of the pink sunsets she often saw on her wanderings in the summer.

Jackie and the Bucket

Inspired by the Aesop story titled The Milkmaid and the Pail

Now I may have mentioned that Jackie can be a bit clumsy, even a bit klutzy. It was amazin' that she made it through each day without seriously damaging somethin' important like her head or one of her limbs. But she never did – not a single broken bone or severe head bump. I also might have made mention that her Ma usually gave her outdoor chores so that Jackie didn't break any more things in the house.

On this particular day Ma did not have anything for Jackie to do, but Jackie kept buggin' her every hour or so for somethin' to do or somethin' to help with. Ma had already suggested she go on a walk, which Jackie did. Jackie always enjoyed walking in the woods that ran along the back of their property.

When Jackie came back, she asked Ma for somethin' else to do. Ma said, "Don't you have any critters or children to take care of?" "Nope," Jackie answered. "Nobody has called."

Ma next asked if she'd played with her hedgehog friend, Harold, yet that day. "Can't," was Jackie's reply. "Can't?" questioned Ma. "Nope, he's off visitin' some friends of his," said Jackie.

So Ma was really scrapin' the bottom of her brain tryin' to think of somethin' for Jackie to do. She reached into the icebox for the milk and realized the bottle was almost empty. That gave her some much needed inspiration.

"Jackie, there is somethin' you can help me with," said Ma. "Yes, Ma?" Jackie asked excitedly. "You know where we keep the milk gatherin' bucket?" "Oh yes, Ma," was Jackie's reply. "Well take it to Farmer Frank's and get it filled only halfway with milk." "Ok, Ma," Jackie responded quickly. "Now Jackie, remember only have it filled halfway so it doesn't spill when you carry it home." "Only halfway, okay Ma."

Off Jackie went to their barn to collect the milk gatherin' bucket and then she started for Farmer Frank's. As she went Jackie hummed the tune "Oh My Darlin' Clementine." In no time at all she was at Farmer Frank's.

Having remembered to ask for only a half bucket full of milk and proud of herself for doing so, Jackie started for home. To occupy herself she kept switchin' the bucket back and forth from her right hand to her left hand until she had an idea. She put the bucket on top of her head. It was quite comfortable, and she kept it steady by lightly placing her left hand on it. As she continued on her way she started thinking about Farmer Frank and the milk.

If Ma and Pa bought a milk cow, then they could sell any milk the family didn't use. With the money from the milk they could buy a chicken. When they sold the eggs from the chicken, Jackie would have the money to buy more material so Ma could make her a new dress (something she'd been interested in after the barn dance she'd attended with Homer). A smile broke out on her face remembering the fun she'd had at the dance. Jackie began humming a tune as she reached up with both arms to dance with her invisible Homer.

And that's when it happened. The milk gatherin' bucket fell off her head, spilled all over her overalls and her bare feet. Now most people would have been terribly upset, but this was a minor event in Jackie's life. She just picked up the bucket and headed back to Farmer Frank's!

Bedtime Stories for Jack and Jackie

When you were little, did your Ma or Pa or Grammy or Grampa read a story or two to you at bedtime? Perhaps you had an older brother or sister who took on the task?

Well, when Jack and Jackie were young'uns their Ma would tell them stories. You see, they didn't have the extra cash money to buy any books and the book mobile wasn't in existence until Jackie and Jack were much older.

Ma had quite the gift for tellin' stories. And these were like no other stories you'd heard before because she'd take a tale she'd heard as a child and put her own twist on it.

Here are a few of the stories that Ma shared with Jack and Jackie when they were just knee high to some grasshoppers.

The Boy Who Cried Coyote

As told by Jackie and Jack's Ma (written by Teri Lott)
Inspired by The Boy Who Cried Wolf

Now Billy's family raised sheep and goats. Monday through Friday, Billy went to school and his Ma took the sheep and goats up the hill just outside their town to eat the luscious, tall, green grass. She had to stand guard of the sheep and goats because there were coyotes all around. But on the weekends, Ma needed to do the washin', cleanin', and mendin', and such and so Billy had the chore of takin' the sheep and goats up the hill.

Since Billy was still a young'un, he took a drum with him to bang in case he saw any coyotes. He had to get up when the sun came up, herd the animals out of town and up the hill. He stayed up on the hill on guard 'til suppertime when he would herd the animals down the hill and back home. Billy thought it was borin'- no fun at all.

Now on one particular Saturday, Billy could hear the other kids playin' baseball. He so wanted to join in that game. So he did somethin' he shouldn't have oughtn'. He started bangin' his drum and yellin' "Coyotes, coyotes!"

Well right away his Ma and his Pa stopped what they were doin'. Ma grabbed her broom and Pa grabbed his shovel. Some neighbors joined them, and they all ran up the hill ready to battle those coyotes. When they reached the top of the hill they looked all around and saw no coyotes.

Grumblin', the others shook their heads at Billy and went back down the hill. Pa went back to workin' on the tractor he was repairin' for another farmer. Ma stayed behind to talk some sense into Billy. "Now Billy," she began, "you know how important it is to this family that you watch these animals on the weekends." Billy hung his head as low as a snake's belly while Ma continued. Shakin' her head and her finger at him she said, "Don't you ever cry coyote when there ain't no coyotes again!"

39

A few weekends later, on a Sunday after church, Billy took those animals up the hill again. They immediately began eatin' that luscious, tall, green grass. Billy began hearin' the other kids pickin' sides to play Hide and Seek. Now Billy wanted to join that game so badly that he picked up his drum – and you know what he did, right? He began to bang that drum and called out, "Coyotes, coyotes!"

Well right away his Ma and his Pa stopped what they were doin'. Once again Ma grabbed her broom and Pa grabbed his shovel. Once again some neighbors joined them, and they all ran up the hill ready to battle those coyotes. When they reached the top of the hill they looked all around and saw no coyotes.

Pa and the others gave Billy a mean look and went back down the hill. Ma stayed behind. Shakin' her head again and shakin' her finger at him again she said, "Now Billy, I already told ya. Don't yell out coyotes when there ain't no coyotes!"

Well that very next Saturday Billy was – well you know where he was – and he fell asleep while watchin' the animals. After all, it was a rather borin' job. Billy turned over and bumped his head on a rock which woke him up. He stretched and opened his eyes just in time to see a pack of coyotes that had started eating some of the sheep and goats.

He grabbed his drum and began bangin' it. "Coyotes, coyotes!" he yelled. No one came. The coyotes ate some more sheep and goats. Billy banged harder on the drum and screamed, "Coyotes, coyotes!" But no one came.

The coyotes got closer and closer to Billy. In desperation, he banged the drum harder than he had ever done before. He screamed until his voice gave out, "Coyotes, there really are coyotes!" "Coyotes…" "Coyo…"

But still no one came. The drum stopped banging. The yellin' stopped. And I'm sad to tell ya, that was the end of Ma and Pa's sheep, the end of Ma and Pa's goats, and the end of Billy. But there sure were some fat coyotes left in those parts!

40

Candylocks and the Three Raccoons

As told by Jackie and Jack's Ma (written by Teri Lott)
Inspired by The Three Bears

Once upon a time there was a family of three raccoons – the Pa, the Ma, and the baby. They lived in the hollowed-out part of a tree.

Each mornin' the mommy raccoon would make all of them some delicious oatmeal. While she worked, she would say, "Pease oatmeal hot. Please oatmeal cold. Pease oatmeal in the pot nine days old. Pa likes it hot. I like it cold. Baby likes it from the pot nine days old."

Then she would put a big bowl with extremely hot oatmeal with berries on the table for Pa. Then she'd add lots of sugar to a middle-sized bowl of cold oatmeal with berries on the table for herself. She liked it sweet. And lastly, she'd put a small bowl of oatmeal with berries on the table for baby.

She'd call out to her family by singing this song: "Good mornin' to you. Good mornin' to you. There's oatmeal at our places. Let me see your happy faces. And this is the way we start a new day." Pa Raccoon would come into the kitchen with the baby on his shoulders. "Let's go on our before-breakfast walk!" he would always announce.

So they left their hollow in the tree and began their walk. Just after they left, who came along but a girl named Candylocks. Her real name was Harper, but everyone called her Candylocks because when she ate candy – which was most of the day – she weren't careful and some of it would get stuck in her long braids.

Well, Candylocks had been walkin' through the woods when the smell of that oatmeal reached her nose. Candylocks said, "Ummm... that smells good." and she went inside the Raccoon's home in the tree. That's when she saw the three bowls of oatmeal on the table.

Since her stomach was growlin' and no one seemed to be around, she decided to eat. She picked up a spoon and tried Pa's oatmeal. It

41

was so hot she spit some of it out sayin', "Ouch, that's too hot and the berries are sour!" Then she tried Ma's oatmeal. She made a face sayin', "Yuck, that's too cold and it's too sweet!" She tried some oatmeal and berries from the third bowl. "Yum, this one is just right," And she proceeded to eat every bit, even licking the bowl clean.

Now Candylocks had been walkin' in the woods for awhile and she was plumb tired out. She saw the Raccoon family's three chairs. She sat down on Pa's chair but immediately got up, sayin', "Ouch, this chair is too hard!" She tried Ma's chair. She found herself sinkin' down, down, down. "Help! I'm bein' swallowed up! This chair is too soft!" Luckily, she was able to get up out of the chair on her own. Then she went over to Baby's chair. "Ahh… this is just right and look my favorite book is right here too!"

Candylocks found a piece of candy in her pocket, stuck it in her mouth and began to read. But the reading made her feel sleepy. So she went searching for a bedroom. She laid down on Pa's bed. Now Pa had a bad back, so his mattress was very firm. Once again Candylocks proclaimed, "Ouch, this is too hard!"

Next, she laid down on Ma's bed. Now Ma liked to be comfortable at night, so her mattress was extra fluffy – full of feathers. Once again Candylocks felt like she was being swallowed up and said, "This is too soft!"

One bed was left. She laid down on Baby's bed which was just right, but before she could even say that she was fast asleep.

The three Raccoons came home from their morning walk ready to eat their oatmeal. They sat down at the table and immediately noticed that someone had been eating their breakfast. Pa announced, "Someone has been eatin' our oatmeal alright." Baby cried, "Mine's all gone!"

Pa declared, "Let's see what's goin' on here." He led his family to their three chairs. Right away they noticed their chairs were out of place and Baby even found his favorite book sitting right on top of his chair which is not where he had left it. Pa announced, "Someone has been sittin' in our chairs alright."

So Pa led them to their bedrooms. Pa saw the wrinkles in his bedspread. Ma saw the wrinkles in her quilt. Before Pa could announce the obvious, Baby cried, "I know someone's been on my bed because she's still here!"

The Raccoon family surrounded Baby's bed. Baby said in a whispered voice, "Look Ma. Look Pa. There's candy in her hair!" At this Candylocks woke up. At first, she was a bit startled, but she quickly recovered and smiled at Baby Raccoon and said, "Hi, I'm Candylocks. I'm sorry to have eaten your oatmeal but I was so very hungry, and you weren't home." Ma Raccoon smiled and said, "It's okay this time, we have plenty, but you really shouldn't stay in someone's home when they aren't there. After all, we might have been dangerous – like some lions or tigers or bears!"

Candylocks became friends with the Raccoon family, and she often went on their morning walks with them and afterwards shared some delicious oatmeal!

Jackie Tales

What Really Happened to the Three Little Owls

As told by Jackie and Jack's Ma (written by Teri Lott)
Inspired by The Three Little Pigs

Mama Owl was cryin'. You see her three almost grown-up daughters were getting' ready to make their own homes and begin their own families. She knew it was time for them to go, a bit past time actually, but it still made her sad.

She gave them each a feathery hug and some motherly advice. "Remember dear ones," she lovingly advised, "Choose strong, tall trees. Watch out for bobcats, foxes, and wolves. Be happy. And remember that I'll love you forever and always."

The oldest sister who had feathers as white as the snow and was called Snowflake, left their mama first. She was excited to be startin' out on her own. She gave her mama a hug and said goodbye. "I love you," Snowflake called as she flew away. "I love you more," her mama replied.

Snowflake flew quite awhile lookin' for the perfect tree to be her new home. She finally spotted a tall, strong oak tree. This would be her home. Excitedly she flew down and began to build her nest.

The middle sister, Ashley, so called because her gray feathers looked like the ashes left after a fire goes out, left their mama a short time later. She was happy to be startin' out on her own. Ashley gave her mama a hug and said goodbye. "I love you," she told her mama. "I love you more," her mama replied.

Ashley flew for a short while until she spotted a beautiful evergreen tree. It swayed a bit in the wind, but that just made it even more beautiful to her. You see Ashley was extremely interested in how things, includin' herself, looked. Ashley swooped down and made her new home in its gorgeous green branches.

44

That left Brownie, the youngest owl. As you probably have guessed, she got her name because she was brown feathers from the top of her head to the tip of her toes. Brownie was impatient to be on her own. As the youngest of the three, she was tired of being "the baby".

She told her mama a quick goodbye and a rushed "I love you." "I love you more," her mama replied. But by then the impatient Brownie was too far away to hear her.

Brownie flew for the shortest while and when she spotted a hawk's nest that had fallen at the base of a strong oak tree, she flew down. Now you might think she'd be okay if she took the nest up into that tall, strong oak but she was so tired she slept in that nest on the ground.

Nearby was an underground burrow where Frankie F. Fox lived. The F usually stood for furry and fun-loving but today it stood for fed up. You see, Frankie had a weak immune system and whenever someone even sneezed in the woods Frankie would catch a cold. He also had hay fever which means he was sneezing, had a runny nose and itchy, watery eyes.

Frankie had noticed he had a new neighbor and was hoping the neighbor would have eye drops for his big, itchy eyes. He thought it was strange that this brown owl had its nest on the ground, but it takes all kinds, right? He went right up to the nest when a big sneeze came on. "Ah, ah, ah, choo!" The owl woke up and stumbled right into the boggy area near her nest. Frankie tried to reach her, but he had a hard time seeing with his watery eyes and then she was gone.

Now Frankie was sad about this, but his eyes were still watery, and he needed those drops even more than before. He had noticed another new neighbor in a nearby evergreen tree. So he stumbled toward the tree and bumped right into it! The tree swayed and swayed. The gray owl fell out of the tree, and she was a goner for sure. Frankie felt for a pulse to make sure. Nothing. He remembered his mama telling him, "Feed a cold, starve a fever." He didn't have a fever; he had a cold so… he ate the gray owl.

Frankie's stomach felt better, but his eyes were still itchy, so he headed over to the oak tree where he had seen another neighbor – a white owl - move in. The neighborhood was sure getting' crowded, especially with owls!

Just as Frankie reached the tall, strong oak tree that was Snowflake's home, Snowflake stepped out onto one of the lower branches and said, "I'd like to talk to you about my sisters." "Your sisters?" Frankie replied with a gulp. "Yes, my sisters." "Oh, so you know what happened?" "Believe me, I hear things," Snowflake responded. "Yeah, I've heard that about owls," said Frankie. "But I don't think you heard the true story. It…it was all an accident. Your first sister…" "Brownie," Snowflake interrupted standing with her wings on her hips. "Oh, okay, Brownie. She was startled by my sneeze. You see I have a cold and hay fever, and she fell into the bog. Then the other sister…" "Ashley," Snowflake interrupted again, shifting her weight a bit. "Oh, ok, Ashley. She just fell out of her tree when I bumped it. My eyes were tearing so much, I didn't even notice that evergreen. I'm not sure that was the best tree for her to pick, was it? I mean look at you, you chose this nice, strong oak tree-

Just then Mother Owl stepped out from behind Snowflake on the same branch. "So you're blamin' all of this on a cold and hay fever?" she said in an angry tone. "And you felt justified to eat my sister?" asked Snowflake just as angrily. "Well…uh…um," replied Frankie as Mother Owl and Snowflake swooped down and began to hit Frankie with their wings. Then they pecked Frankie on the head with their beaks.

How did Frankie respond? Well he howled and ran away as fast as his legs would carry him. Frankie F. Fox was never seen in that part of the woods again!

Naomi and the Wolf

As told by Jackie and Jack's Ma (written by Teri Lott)
Inspired by Little Red Riding Hood

Once upon a time there was a little girl named Naomi. She was a happy girl with a big smile. And she loved to sing. Her favorite song was "If You're Happy and You Know It." Everybody loved Naomi and she loved everyone.

One afternoon, Naomi's mama asked her to take a basket to her grammy. You see, Naomi's grammy was sick. In the basket were delicious cookies – yum, yum. Her mama told her to be careful and not get off the path that led to grammy's house.

So off Naomi went to her grammy's house. She sang as she skipped. "If you're happy and you know it clap your hands. If you're happy and you know it clap your hands. If you're happy and you know it, then your face will surely show it. If you're happy and you know it clap your hands." Since Naomi couldn't clap her hands and hold the basket at the same time, the song wasn't as fun as it usually was.

Naomi continued skipping and changed her song to one that she had made up herself. She sang, "I'm goin' to my grammy's house, my grammy's house, my grammy's house. I'm goin' to my grammy's house 'cause she is sick."

Wouldn't you know it? A wolf heard Naomi's song, so he knew exactly what was goin' on. He hid behind some bushes. He was plannin' to jump out and eat Naomi and then he could go and eat her grammy too!

He waited until Naomi skipped past the bush. He jumped out. Naomi didn't scream, she didn't run, she didn't even tremble. Instead she smiled at him and said, "Oh hi! Would you like a cookie? They're very good. I helped my mama make them."

47

Well no one had ever offered a cookie to the wolf before. He ate one and said, "Yum." Then he turned and ran into the woods. I don't think anyone ever saw that wolf again.

And Naomi? Well she shrugged, then continued skippin' to her grammy's house. When she got there, she found out that her grammy was feelin' better. They sat on her grammy's bed and ate cookies and drank milk together.

Stories written by our Jackie (and Teri Lott)

As you might recall in the story ***Summertime and the Livin's Easy, or Is It?*** Jackie started her own business takin' care of other people's critters and kids. Durin' that time, Jackie also started to write some stories to entertain the kids she was watchin'.

Followin' are a few of the stories that Jackie wrote. Some are for younger kiddos and some are for the older ones. But they are pretty good stories, so I think all ages can enjoy them.

I think you'll agree with me that Jackie just might have a future in writin' stories. Who knows, maybe someday she'll be a real author and her stories will be in a book.

Louisa, the Lightning Bug

Written by Jackie (and Teri Lott)

Night had fallen. The moon was shinin' so brightly it woke Louisa up. The first thing she heard was, "grumble, grumble." The sound was comin' from her stomach. Boy was Louisa hungry! She shot off the leaf she'd been sleepin' on and began to search for the closest source of nectar. She smacked her lips in anticipation. Just as suddenly as she had left her bed, she realized somethin' wasn't right.

She took a moment to take in her surroundings. First, she looked left, then she looked right, then she looked up, and then she looked down. Everything looked just as it should. Then she listened intently, but except for the grumblin' sounds from her own protestin' stomach, nothin' sounded amiss, nothin' sounded wrong. Then she realized what was different, what was out of place, what wasn't quite right – it was her! Her taillight was not on!

Louisa could not understand what had happened. She felt a bit sad. She felt a bit mad. And, well, she felt a bit bad. And when you are upset or frustrated, you don't feel like eatin'. That's how Louisa felt too. All she could think about now was her broken taillight. What could have caused this? What made this happen? It was glowin' just fine last night. "Oh my, oh my! What can I do? What can I try?" thought Louisa.

"What's the matter? Why so glum chum?" said a voice. It was a raccoon, Louisa's friend. "Oh Rascal, my taillight isn't workin' – see?!?" Louisa moved closer so he could see, or rather not see, the light. "Hmm. Has this ever happened before?" asked Rascal. "No never. Oh my, oh my. What can I do? What can I try?" said Louisa. "Do you need your light to fly?" inquired the raccoon. "Oh no, I just don't feel right. I don't feel like me. I feel a bit sad, a bit mad, and a bit bad," said Louisa.

"Well maybe you're too upset, you're stressed out. Let me give you a neck rub," said Rascal. Louisa said, "That would be great, thanks!" So Rascal gave Louisa a neck rub. It felt great and she felt more relaxed. But her taillight was still out. "Thanks, anyway," Louisa told her friend. "Well, good luck," said Rascal. "I've got some garbage cans to look in to!"

Louisa took off flyin' all the while saying, "Oh my, oh my. What can I do? What can I try?" "Riddup, riddup," she heard from below. She flew closer to the sound and saw her friend Frog sitting on a log by the edge of the pond. "What's up buttercup?" Frog asked. "Oh, Frog, my taillight isn't workin'. I feel a bit sad, a bit mad, and a bit bad." "Riddup, riddup, are you sure its not just covered with pollen from those flowers you sit on?" "I guess it could be," replied Louisa.

"Well," said Frog, "I can splash some water on it." "As long as its not any trouble," said Louisa. "No trouble at all, I love jumpin' into the water, you know. Just come a little closer," said Frog. So, with her hopes high, Louisa swooped down. Frog jumped into the pond and water splashed all over Louisa's taillight. They both looked in anticipation, but nothing' had changed. "Thanks for trying," said Louisa. But Frog had already hopped off.

"Oh my, oh my. What can I do? What can I try?" Louisa said as she rose in the air. "Hoo, hoo. What's wrong with you?" Louisa looked up and saw Owl in the oak tree "Oh, hi Owl. My taillight isn't workin'." "What have you tried, hoo, hoo?" Louisa said, "Rascal Raccoon gave me a neck rub to relax me and Frog tried to wash off the pollen on it – but nothing worked. Maybe it's broken." "Hoo, hoo. Perhaps, perhaps not," said Owl. "Maybe the Enchanted Tree would have an idea for you. Hoo, hoo." "That's a great idea. Thanks Owl!" said Louisa.

Louisa flew as fast as she could to the Enchanted Tree. She couldn't believe she hadn't thought of this idea herself. The Enchanted Tree was very smart and very kind. She was a bit nervous when she got to the tree. He had his eyes closed. She wondered, was he sleepin'? Was he thinkin'? She just hovered in front of him and didn't say a word.

After a short time, the magnificent tree said, "Good evenin', Louisa. You look different tonight. Are your wearing your antennae differently?" he asked with a chuckle. Louisa said, "No, it's my taillight. It isn't workin'. It makes me fell a bit sad, a bit mad and a bit bad. I also feel strange." The Enchanted Tree replied in his deep voice, "It is hard to feel different. Believe me, I understand. But think of all the blessings you have. Say them aloud and you'll feel better."

Louisa wasn't convinced that this would work, but she was willin' to give anything a try. "Okay. Let's see. I'm happy that I am healthy- except for my taillight." And do you know, she felt a little less sad, a little less mad and a little less bad. "I'm also thankful there are plenty of flowers, so I have nectar and pollen to eat." And she felt even less sad, less mad, and less bad. Then thinking of Rascal Raccoon, Frog and Owl, she said, "I'm very thankful to have such good friends." That final blessing put a big smile on her face. And then a wonderful thing happened! An amazing thing happened! A truly terrific thing happened! Her light came on! "Thanks, Mr. Tree. I'll remember my blessings from now on!"

As Louisa flew off with her taillight glowin', she sang, "I get by with a little help from my friends. I got my light with a little help from my friends. I'm flyin' bright with a little help from my friends!"

So if you ever have a problem, somethin' that makes you feel a little bit sad, a little bit mad or a little bit sad, ask your friends or family for help just like Louisa did.

The Colors of the Ocean

Written by Jackie (and Teri Lott)

When the world first began, the oceans were all the same color – a murky green. And everythin' in the oceans were the same color – a murky green. The water was murky green, the shells and rocks were murky green, the oceans' bottoms were murky green, the coral reefs were murky green and all the animals in the sea were murky green. The fish, the dolphins, the whales, the sharks, and all the other creatures were…murky green.

And then somethin' happened, a marvelous thing. A baby fish was born, and it was not murky green – it was pink! Her mother named her Rosita, which means little rose or little pink. Everyone who saw Rosita was amazed that somethin' that lived in the dull green ocean was such a beautiful, splendiferous color.

As Rosita got older, she began to wonder why she was the only thing in the ocean that was not murky green. She liked the bright color of her scales, but she felt very different from everythin' else in her world – like a fish out of water! So Rosita began askin' the other sea dwellers if they liked being green.

She asked her best friend, a fish named Marmalade because he loved jelly, how he liked bein' green. "I don't know, Rosita, I was born this color, so I haven't thought about it much." Then he paused to consider her question. "I guess if I had the chance to be another color, I'd like to be orange like my favorite jelly."

Next Rosita asked a dolphin she knew. "Oh, I've thought about bein' a different color ever since you were born," replied the dolphin. "I'd like to be blue. Blue like the afternoon sky. But it doesn't matter, I've been this green color since I birth and there's no changin' it."

Then Rosita went over to a lobster bed. There she found a father lobster and his son. She asked them how they felt about bein' green. "It's what I'm used to," answered the father. "I don't like it at all," piped up his young son. "I'd like to be red like the color of the sky when the sun goes down."

Almost every sea creature that Rosita spoke to wished they could be another color. Even Simon the shark wanted to be gray instead of green. Not a big color change, but a change.

Rosita decided she wanted to help all of her friends. She became a fish on a mission. But she had no idea where to begin. She swam around back and forth, forth and back. This is what she did when she was thinkin'. Suddenly inspiration hit – she knew what to do next. She knew the first step of her mission – her mission to bring color to the ocean.

Rosita swam as fast as her fins would take her, swimmin' faster than she had ever done in her young life. She was swimmin' to the one creature of the sea who might have the answer to her quest, the person many of us go to when we need answers – her mom. "Mom, mom, mom," she called out breathlessly as she approached their home. "Rosita, my sweet," her mom responded. "It is so good to see you, but slow down and take a deep breath." So Rosita inhaled and filled her gills. Then she exhaled. She was calmer now.

"Mom, I have something important to talk to you about," she finally continued. "All right my little one, I'm listenin'." "Mom, do you know why I was born pink and not green?" "Ahhh... I thought one day you would ask me this question. Well, I was tired of everythin' around us bein' the same so wished on a star that you would be born a different color. And it worked!" "Which star in the sky did you wish on?" Rosita asked. "Not a sky star," her mom answered. "A starfish. I've wished on starfishes since I was a little girl."

"I've done that with you, mom, but none of my wishes have come true." "This is my only wish that did and I think it's for three reasons." "Yes, mom, I'm listenin'," said Rosita. And she was listenin' intently – listenin' with every scale on her rosy body. "First, I think it's because I wanted it more than anythin'. I also think the ocean itself decided it was time for a change. And I wished on a special starfish, one that had a broken arm."

"Mom, some of my friends want to be a different color. Do you think the ocean is ready for more color?" "Rosita, I do not pretend to know what the ocean wants. But it wouldn't hurt to try," Rosita said, "If only I can find that special starfish." Her mom smiled and said, "Before you go on your search, Rosita, let me give you somethin'." Rosita's mom turned tail and swam into a small cave. When she came out, she had the special starfish – the one with the broken arm. "Here you go," her mom said smilin'.

"Oh, wow Mom! This is great!" Rosita looked at the special starfish in awe. "Well, are you going to try it out?" her mom asked excitedly. "Oh, uh, yes," Rosita responded. "I guess I'll start with Marmalade. He wants to be orange." Rosita closed her eyes and wished with all her heart and soul. Then she opened them and said, "I guess I'll go find Marmalade and see if it worked." "Ok, dear. I'll wait right here for your report," her mom said with a smile.

Rosita hadn't swum very far when she and her mom heard an exuberant voice yelling, "Rosita, Rosita, Rosita!!!!" She recognized it as Marmalade's voice, but she did not recognize her friend. Marmalade was orange – orange with white and black stripes. "Did you do this, Rosita?" Marmalade asked while he swam excitedly around Rosita and her mom. "I..I..I guess so," she responded. "It's great! It's fantastic! It's wonderful!" Marmalade screamed and grabbed Rosita's fin and spun her around. All of them started laughin' with joy.

And after that, it was just a matter of Rosita askin' each of her friends if they'd like to change colors and using her special starfish. The dolphin became blue, the shark gray, the young lobster red. And when his father saw the brilliant color of his son, he asked to be red too. Soon the ocean was full of color. There was still murky green in places, but not in all the places. It is the ocean that we know today.

Ginny, the Trickster

Written by Jackie (and Teri Lott)

Her name was Virginia, but her friends and family had always called her Ginny. "Ginny with a G, that's me," she would say. And since Ginny was so friendly and kind, she made friends quickly so only friends she hadn't made yet called her Virginia.

Not only was Ginny kind and friendly to everyone she met, but she was also blessed with the ability to cook anythin' you would want. French, German, Italian – any kind of cuisine. And she would fix it to perfection.

Although Ginny was an excellent cook, she was a messy cook. She moved from one task to another spillin' a bit here, droppin' a bit there. She didn't even notice it she was so busy. Then after the meal was cookin' in the oven or on the stovetop, then and only then she would clean up.

One chilly winter day Ginny had some time on her hands, so she decided to make one of her favorite meals – spaghetti and meatballs. Ginny made everythin' from scratch – the meatballs, the spaghetti sauce, and the pasta. It took hours and hours to make all of this so Ginny always made extra to give to friends or to keep for another time.

While Ginny was workin', she did not notice that some of her yummy noodles fell to the floor, rolled across the kitchen floor, out the door, across the back porch, down the steps, across the yard and down into a hole at the base of an oak tree. You see, Ginny lived in southern Ohio in the foothills of the Appalachian Mountains and her yard sloped down away from her house.

Next, unnoticed by Ginny, several spoonfuls of her delicious sauce fell to the floor, spread across the kitchen floor, out the door, across the back porch, down the steps, across the yard and down into that same hole.

Then when Ginny was makin' her meatballs, a few fell off the countertop. Ginny happened to notice the missin' meatballs and looked down just in time to see one of them roll across the kitchen floor and out the door. Ginny was surprised and opened the door to see where the meatball was goin'. It went across the back porch and down the steps. So Ginny followed. The meatball continued across the yard and went down into a hole at the base of the tree.

Ginny was so surprised that she bent down to look in that hole. She couldn't see anythin', so she got down on her hands and knees to look – not because she planned to eat a meatball that had rolled across a floor, a porch, and a yard – yuck – but because she was curious. After all wouldn't you be?

The next thing she knew she felt a slight pressure – like you might feel when you're on a plane and it changes altitude – and then she found herself being pulled downward. She realized she was in a hole below the ground. It wasn't very large – the ceilin' if that's what you'd call it – was low. She was fine sittin' up, but she could not stand. Before she could gather her wits, she saw a small creature standin' in front of her and grinnin'. The creature had long green curly hair goin' down its back and strange multicolored bumps all over its body.

"Are you the lady who makes all the delicious, delectable food?" the creature asked. Ginny nodded her head yes while continuin' to move her gaze from his? hers? its? head down to its feet. "Oh, where are my manners," the creature said. "My name is Mordy and I am a Morlucky." "A Morlucky?" Ginny said finally findin' her voice. "Yes, a Morlucky. Perhaps you've seen a movie in which there is a group of underground dwellers called the Morlocks. We are descendants of the Morlocks." Now Ginny was a movie buff, and she knew that this creature, Mordy – was that its name – was talkin' about the movie *The Time Machine* that was based on a book by HG Wells. Rackin' her brain she realized that the Morlocks ate people in that movie.

Her face must have shown what she was thinkin'. And Mordy said, "Oh, we don't eat people anymore. Not when we can get food as wonderful as yours." "Oh, that's good," said Ginny as she looked around trying to find a way to escape. "And now you are gonna to cook for us," Mordy announced. "Oh I couldn't possibly," Ginny replied. "Why not? We know you give your food to other people, so why not us?" "Umm... because I need my kitchen to cook in," Ginny said.

"We have a lovely kitchen," Mordy said as he waved his hand. Suddenly the ceilin' raised and to her right, Ginny saw a fully equipped kitchen. "Besides," Mordy said with a wide grin that showed his broken, gray teeth, "you really don't have a choice."

So that was that. Or was it? Ginny went into the kitchen and was told she needed to begin by making pasta. You see Ginny's pasta was so good you could eat it plain, besides Mordy and his friends had never put all of the bits and pieces that fell into their hole together. Mordy told Ginny to get to work and then he disappeared.

Ginny had made her pasta so often; she began makin' it using rote memory as her brain worked on a way out of this. The solution was simple – she needed to get out of that hole and back into her house. But how? Then a plan came to her. She added hot pepper flakes to the pasta. When it was done, she called out "Uh, Mordy, the pasta is ready."

He immediately appeared, saw the big plate on the counter, smiled from ear to ear – or at least what Ginny thought were his ears – and took a big bite. "WHEW WEE!" he screamed. "That's' not right, that's not right!" "Well," Ginny said, "This is not my own kitchen so I may have done somethin' wrong. If you just let me cook in my own kitchen…" But Mordy interrupted and said, "NO! Forget the pasta. Make some of your yummy sauce." Again he disappeared.

Again Ginny began to make the sauce, but instead of tomatoes she used strawberries and raspberries that she crushed. When it was nice and hot, she called out, "Mordy the sauce is ready." Again he immediately appeared, grabbed a big spoon, and took a big bite. "YUCK! This is too sweet. It's not right, it's not right!" "Well," Ginny said, "If I could just cook in my own kitchen." "NO! yelled Mordy. "Forget the sauce, make some scrumptious meatballs. Those are a meal in themselves." And yet again he disappeared.

Ginny began mixin' ingredients for the meatballs. She had several special ingredients to make them so scrumptious, but she substituted one of them for crushed up pebbles. She called for Mordy and when he appeared he grabbed a fork, cut the huge meatball in half, and stuffed it all into his mouth. "OWWWW! I think I broke some teeth! These don't taste right!" screamed Mordy. "Well I don't think it would take much to break your teeth, they're in terrible shape," Ginny replied. "You try getting' a dentist to work on your teeth when you live underground and you're a cousin to a Morlock," Mordy replied sadly.

Just then Ginny realized that Mordy and his family and friends must truly live a difficult life and so she proposed a deal. The Morlucky's would let her return to her home, and she would supply them with delicious, delectable food. And since then the Morluckys have truly felt lucky to have met Ginny.

How Pelican Got His Pouch

Written by Jackie (and Teri Lott)

Once, forever and a day ago, Pelican had the same kind of beak the other birds have today. Their beaks were long and slender.

Now robins used their beaks to eat blueberries and worms. They also sang beautiful songs.

Ostriches used their beaks to eat seeds, grass, and flowers. They could go without drinking water for several days.

Parrots' beaks were a bit shorter, and they used them to help themselves climb up a tree. They also used their beaks to crush the shells of seeds.

Chickens used their beaks to pick up bugs and seeds. They laid eggs for folks to eat, too!

Owls' short, curved beaks were used for hunting their food. And they could move their heads nearly all the way around.

Ducks had wide, flat beaks they used to find and grab their food of plants and fish. They swam beautifully, as well.

Penguins had long, slim beaks they used to catch fish. Their wonderful, webbed feet helped them to swim.

That brings us to Pelican. Pelican's small beak was only good for catching small fish and he had no other special talents. He became jealous of the other birds. He wanted to be more like them. So Pelican started telling stories about the other birds. But those stories were lies so none of them were true.

One of the songbirds went to Mother Nature and told her what Pelican was doing. Mother Nature was terribly upset with Pelican. She called for him, then she warned him that if he did not stop telling lies about the other birds, she would make his beak grow all out of shape. Pelican promised not to tell any more stories. He didn't want a misshaped beak that the other birds would laugh at. As he left Mother Nature she gave him this reminder, "If your lies do not stop. The bottom of your beak will drop and drop."

Unfortunately, Pelican did not keep his promise. First, he told everyone that Chicken was hiding his eggs. Of course he wasn't. A fox had eaten all the eggs. As soon as Pelican had told everyone, his beak got bigger!

Then he told everyone that Duck was eating all the fish in the pond – another lie! Actually Pelican himself had pulled the fish out of the pond. Well, his beak got even bigger!

Pelican then told everyone that Owl was putting mice in the farmer's house. Of course he wasn't, mice were just getting in. And Pelican's beak got much bigger! It was really big now!

Pelican called out for Mother Nature, but there was no answer. He called again this time saying he was sorry for telling stories. Mother Nature answered. She said she'd consider his plight after he apologized to each of the other birds.

So Pelican went to each bird to apologize. To Chicken he said, "I'm sorry I said you hid the eggs. I knew that Fox had taken them. I'll never say somethin' like that again." Chicken replied, "Cluck, cluck. All right. Just see that you don't."

He went to Duck and said, "I'm sorry I said you were eating all the fish. I took the fish. I'll never do it again." Duck responded, "Quack, quack. All right, just see that you don't."

Finally he went to Owl and said, "I'm sorry I said you put mice in the farmer's house. I will never say it again." Owl said, "Hoo, hoo. All right, just see that you don't."

Pelican returned to Mother Nature. She told him she was happy that he had apologized to all the birds and felt he had learned his lesson. Pelican smiled. Mother Nature continued, "But, I think keeping your beak this way will remind you not to tell lies about others anymore." Pelican was disappointed and got ready to leave.

But Mother Nature said she had a piece of advice for him. With a wink and a smile she said, "You should go and catch some fish." Pelican thought this was a strange thing for Mother Nature to say, but he was hungry, so he did head out to catch some fish.

Well, Pelican had a wonderful surprise in store for him. For he discovered that he could actually catch more fish with his new beak! The fish he caught could rest safely in his pouch while he fished for more. Since then, all Pelicans have such pouches below their beaks but not one of them tells lies about other birds.

The Tale of Blackie

Written by Jackie (and Teri Lott)

The critter I'm about to tell you about didn't really have a name. The other critters called him Blackie, because, well because he wore a furry black coat.

Now this critter I'm about to tell you about didn't have much in the way of protection from his enemies – Owl, Fox, and Bobcat – except that his furry dark coat helped him to hide in the darkness of the wood and the darkness of night. His legs weren't of much use as they were short. Why he could only run nine mph for a short distance if he tried with all his might. He didn't see very well either – only about ten feet away. But he had excellent smelling and hearing powers, so he used them to find his food.

I bet you're wondering what kind of food he liked. Well, he'd eat insects, frogs, snakes, eggs, berries, leaves, roots, and nuts. He's what those science people call omnivorous – he'd eat just about anything.

Well the particular day I want to tell you about – well it wasn't really daytime it was dusk and just starting to get dark. Blackie had been walking slowly along at the edge of the wood looking for worms and grubs. He had some success but was still hungry. He had been so busy walking with his head down looking for his dinner that he hadn't heard Owl's wings until almost the last minute.

Blackie raced as fast as his little legs could carry him and he hid under a large man-made object. His little heart was pounding for quite a while. Finally he risked looking out from under the large object he had hidden under. What he did not know was that it was a hay wagon, and he was near the farmer's kitchen garden.

Now if you don't know what a kitchen garden is – that's where a farmer's wife grows vegetables for the family's use. Well just that day the farmer had painted the wood fence around the garden and the paint was still a bit wet in places.

Blackie left the shelter of the wagon and when he didn't hear Owl's wings any longer, he went back to searching the ground for things to eat. His nose immediately noticed wonderful smells coming from that garden.

Blackie squeezed through two pickets and began taste testing the veggies he found close to the fence. Yum, yum! These were new tastes, and they were good! He didn't know he was eating wild onions, cabbages, and asparagus. All of these may have tasted good to Blackie, but they made his breath smell stinky! As it was getting close to dawn, Blackie squeezed himself back through the two pickets in the fence and went back to his burrow to get some much-needed sleep.

The next evening, Blackie was walking through the woods again searching for food when he heard giggling from some of the other critters. Blackie stopped sniffling the ground and looked up to see what the others were giggling at. He didn't see anything funny and could use a good laugh, so he asked them why they were laughing. No one answered, they just kept laughing. Blackie went over to one of them and asked. "Whew, your breath is awful – it's so stinky!" was the reply. And then, "We're laughing because of your white stripe." "What white stripe?" asked Blackie. "The one down your back," was the answer.

Well this presented quite a problem for Blackie. How would he be able to blend into the black of night and dark of the woods so Owl, Fox and Bobcat could not see him? He began to panic. He couldn't think straight! Then he remembered what the other critter said about his breath. He formed a plan. He went to wise Turtle and explained his idea. Turtle agreed to help.

The following night Blackie went back to the farmer's kitchen garden. He gorged himself with all the onions, cabbage, and asparagus he could find. But he didn't swallow all of it. Some of it he chewed into a mushy mess and put it in the two small sacs that wise Turtle had made for him and strapped on the insides of his hind legs, just under his cushions.

A few days later, Blackie once again had his nose to the ground searching for worms and grubs. Once again, he did not hear Owl approaching. But, when he did, he did not try to run. He did not try to hide. He turned around, lifted his tail, and squeezed his cushions tightly.

Out of those two sacs squirted the stinkiest spray Owl had ever smelled and the spray squirted right into his eyes. Owl took off in a hurry!

And that is why, to this day, Blackie's kin are no longer called Blackie. Those science people call them mephitis, mephitis which means terrible smell, terrible smell. But the rest of us? We call them… skunks!

A note from the author…

Although this is my third book, it still feels strange to call myself an author. As a little girl I thought I'd become a teacher. And after a few bumps along the way, I did become a teacher. Thirty years later, I began a new career as a storyteller.

Then came 2020 and as they say, "When one door closes another one opens." I collected some of my favorite tales and published my first book, *Lots of Tales Stories that Grow with Your Children.* I published its sequel, *Lots of Tales, Too Seasonal Stories that Grow with Your Children,* shortly thereafter.

I have loved Jack Tales since I first heard *Jack and the Beanstalk.* There are many storytellers, me included, who have written original Jack tales as well as retold the oldies but goodies. I began thinking about Jack's family – a family of three boys. What, I thought, if Jack had a sister that none of us ever hear about? So, I started by creating a twin sister for Jack – Jackie. And that was the beginning of this book – *Jackie Tales, the Untold Stories of Jack's Sister.*

I hope you enjoy the stories, and they bring a little sunshine into your life!

For more stories by Teri Lott, visit her website at:

www.lottsoftales.weebly.com

or contact her at:

www.lotts.of.tales@gmail.com

Made in United States
North Haven, CT
05 November 2023

43637349R00045